Photo Credits

World Map: p.6-7: US Department of State (France); Library of Congress/Carol M. Highsmith LC-DIG-highsm-20583 (California); Library of Congress/Carol M. Highsmith LC-DIG-highsm-45295 (New York); Lieutenant Elizabeth Crapo/NOAA (Ecuador); US Department of State (Italy); NASA (United Arab Emirates). **France:** p.14-15: Anastasia Yarmolovich (Mont Saint-Michel); US Department of State (Eiffel Tower, Arc de Triomphe); Joe deSousa; Carrie Garcia. **Morocco:** p.22–23: Peace Corps (Fez); NASA/GSFC/Jeff Schmaltz/MODIS/Rapid Response Team (The Sahara); USAID (Camels); p.24–25 (left to right): Dave Stamboulis (Architecture); Tuul & Bruno Morandi (Museums). **Brazil:** p.32–33: US Department of State (Copacabana Beach); NASA/GSFC/ Jeff Schmaltz/MODIS Land Rapid Response Team (Amazon Rainforest). **UAE:** p.42-43: Susanne Kremer (Emirates Palace Hotel); US Department of State (Sheikh Zayed Grand Mosque); Kairi Aun (Rub' al-Khali); p.44–45: Central Intelligence Agency (Burj Al Arab Hotel); NASA (Palm Jumeirah). **Italy:** p.52: NASA Earth Observatory (Mount Etna); Giampaolo Macorig (Venice); p.53–54: US Department of State (The Colosseum; Vatican City; The Last Supper). **California:** p.62:-63: US Geological Survey (Napa Valley); Library of Congress/Carol M. Highsmith LC-DIG-highsm- 21783 (Redwood Forests); Jonathan Felis, USGS Western Ecological Research Center (Big Sur); p.64: Library of Congress/Carol M. Highsmith LC-DIG-highsm-17941 (San Francisco); Library of Congress/Carol M. Highsmith LC-DIG-highsm-20583 (Golden Gate Bridge); Shutterstock (Cable Cars). **Ecuador:** p.72-73: Lieutenant Elizabeth Crapo/NOAA (Galápagos Islands); Peace Corps (Andes Mountains); Central Intelligence Agency (Quito); p.74–75: Lieutenant Elizabeth Crapo/NOAA (Guayaquil); Dr. Roger Hewett/NOAA NMFS SWFC (Wildlife). **Japan:** p.82–83: Jeff Schmaltz, MODIS Rapid Response Team, NASA/GSFC (Islands); US Department of State (Hiroshima); US Department of State / William Ng (Tokyo); Scott Bauer/USDA (Cherry Blossoms). **Indonesia:** p.90–91: Ali Usman Wahyu Hidayat/NOAA (Java); Peace Corps (Rice Fields); Christoph Kern, USGS (Volcanoes); Tony Djogo, USAID Indonesia (Sumatra); p.92–93: Peace Corps (Pasars); Manjik Pictures (Jakarta). **New York:** p.100-101: NOAA (Long Island); Sheri Phillips, NOAA/NESDIS/NODC/DBMD (Upstate and Western New York); Library of Congress/Carol M. Highsmith LC-DIG-highsm-45295 (Statue of Liberty); p.102-103: Library of Congress/Carol M. Highsmith LC-DIG-highsm-16914 (Times Square); Library of Congress/Carol M. Highsmith LC-DIG-highsm-16915 (Empire State Building); Library of Congress/Carol M. Highsmith LC-DIG-highsm-13116 (Central Park).

hmhbooks.com

Written by Cynthia Platt
Designed by Sarah Boecher
The type was set in Proxima Nova.

ISBN: 978-0-358-05173-2

Manufactured in Malaysia
TWP 10 9 8 7 6 5 4 3 2 1
4500764505

WHERE IN THE WORLD IS
CARMEN SANDIEGO?™

**Fun facts, cool maps, and seek-and-finds
for 10 locations around the world**

A Note to Potential Thieves:

Here's the first thing you should know about me: I am a thief. My name is Carmen Sandiego—and if you've heard about me, it's true: I steal things. But no need to hide your piggy banks: I only steal from the bad guys. I know every trick in the book, because I was raised by an organization called VILE. That's right, just like it sounds. When I found out what that really stands for—Villains' International League of Evil—I hit the road. Now I try to find VILE operatives all around the world to thwart their criminal activities. If there are any profits from my work, I give them to charity. It's a hard job, but somebody's got to do it!

The good news is that I don't have to do it alone. My friend Player always has my back. He's a magician. Not the pull-a-rabbit-out-of-his-hat kind, though he *has* been known to disappear down some internet rabbit holes. Some folks call him a hacker. Like me, he's the good kind. He's got the research and information you need about every place before you go. Player's also got the tech skills to give you *more* than you need to beat VILE at their own game.

Which is super helpful, because VILE is out there, and we all need to watch out for them. Do you have a good eye? Exceptional attention to detail? Good. Because right now, I need you to become part of my team. Your job is to find VILE and to stop them before they can steal treasures and tech from all around the world. VILE operatives will be lurking in every corner. You'll have to be careful and cunning. I'll either be one step ahead of you—or one step behind. You really never know where I'm going to turn up or when, so keep your eyes open.

Player will brief you with all the information you need to chase down VILE and stop them in their tracks. Like I said, it's risky but extremely rewarding work. Not rewarding as in "it pays"—it's rewarding if you enjoy helping people as much as I do. You do? I know—it was never a question in my mind. Welcome to Team Carmen. Now it's your turn.

Carmen Sandiego

Where You're Headed:

FRANCE

CALIFORNIA

NEW YORK

ECUADOR

BRAZIL

MOROCCO

ITALY

JAPAN

INDONESIA

UNITED ARAB EMIRATES

KEEP AN EYE OUT FOR THESE VILE OPERATIVES:

TIGRESS

She might not be an actual tiger, but she's as fierce as one—and those claws are *sharp*.

MIME BOMB

He doesn't say much, but he's a pro at hiding in plain sight—and where you least expect him.

LE CHÈVRE AND EL TOPO

These partners in crime almost always work together. Le Chèvre is an expert climber, while El Topo is a master digger.

PAPERSTAR

Some people create origami to relax. Paperstar makes it to use as weapons. Very deadly weapons.

LADY DOKUSO

She lives up to her name, which means "toxin" in Japanese. The poison darts in her parasol pack a serious punch.

NEAL THE EEL

See a small space where no one could fit? Well, Neal the Eel can, so be on the lookout.

OTTER MAN AND MOOSE BOY

This Scandinavian team has brains (Otter Man) *and* brawn (Moose Boy)—a very bad combination.

FRANCE

FRANCE

Hi! Player here, and I've got your first assignment for you. VILE operatives have been tracked to France, so that's where you'll be heading. Before you get there, though, I wanted to give you some basics about the country so you know what you're getting into.

JUST THE BASICS

Population: about 65 million

Size: 221,345 square miles (549,970 square kilometers) in area

Capital: Paris

Languages: French and some regional languages such as Breton, Basque, and Occitan

SHOW ME THE MONEY

Currency: Euro

Agricultural products: wheat, cereals, sugar beets, potatoes, and wine grapes for their world-famous wine

Industries: machinery, chemicals, automobiles, metallurgy, and aircraft

WHAT'S FOR DINNER?

Escargot: snails cooked in garlic and butter

Cuisse de grenouilles: frog legs

Fromage: cheese—more than 300 varieties

SAY WHAT?

Hello: *bonjour* (good day) or *bonsoir* (good evening)

Goodbye: *au revoir*

Thank you: *merci*

Where is the bathroom?: *Où sont les toilettes?*

FRANCE

Want something a little more specific? Here are some of the big sites around France. VILE might just be heading to one of them.

Mont Saint-Michel

* The Benedictine abbey on the island was founded in AD 966.

* There's a road now, but you used to have to hurry out there on foot during low tide—and hope you didn't get caught midway on the way back.

* Legend states that King Arthur himself once came to the mountain to kill a monstrous giant.

Eiffel Tower

* Originally built for the 1889 World's Fair in Paris and has stood tall ever since

* Tallest structure in the entire world until 1930

* Big tourist attraction: approximately 7 million visitors each year

Arc de Triomphe

* Stands at the western end of Paris's famous Champs-Élysées

* Construction began in 1806 on the order of Napoleon Bonaparte in honor of his armies' victories in battle

* Wasn't finished until 1836, fifteen years after Napoleon died

* After World War I, chosen as the location of France's Tomb of the Unknown Soldier

River Seine

- ✹ Weaves through the heart of Paris
- ✹ Spanned by thirty-seven bridges in Paris alone as it connects the city's Left and Right Banks
- ✹ About 485 miles (780 kilometers) long

Notre-Dame de Paris

- ✹ The first stone for this cathedral was set in 1163, and the final touches weren't completed until nearly two hundred years later.
- ✹ Its three rose windows contain glass from the 1200s.
- ✹ A massive fire broke out on April 15, 2019, destroying the wooden roof and the 300-foot-tall (90-meter-tall) spire.

A precious gemstone has gone missing from an art gallery. But VILE hasn't gotten very far. Now it's up to you to find the missing jewel!

Knight's armor

Rainbow umbrella

Precious gemstone

Police officer with mustache

Pearl necklace

Mime Bomb

Tigress

Decorative vase

That was amazing! But VILE is just getting started. Time to say *au revoir* to France and head to our next destination.

MOROCCO

MOROCCO

Whew—you got to Morocco just in time! My sources are showing that VILE is way ahead of you, so you'll have to act fast.

JUST THE BASICS

Population: about 34 million

Size: 172,317 square miles (446,300 square kilometers) in area

Capital: Rabat

Languages: Arabic (primarily the Darija dialect), Tamazight and other Berber languages, French

WHAT'S THE WEATHER?

While the coast has a Mediterranean climate (hot, dry summers and cool, wet winters), in the interior, the weather can hit extremes in temperature and wind.

SHOW ME THE MONEY

Currency: Moroccan dirham

Agricultural products: barley, wheat, and citrus fruits

Industries: phosphate mining, auto parts, and leather goods

WHAT'S FOR DINNER?

Tagine: stew often made with meat and dried fruit, named after the pot it's cooked in

Coucous: wheat pasta shaped like small grains

Mint tea: sweet gunpowder tea steeped in boiled water with mint leaves

SAY WHAT?

Hello:
saalam uwaleekum
(peace be upon you)

Thank you:
shukran

Goodbye:
besslama or *ma'assalama*

Yes:
iyah

No:
ila

Maybe:
imken

DANGERS

Creatures:
horned viper, scorpions

MOROCCO

Now that you've got the basics, let's look at some of the places in Morocco that VILE might be targeting.

Casablanca

* Morocco's largest city and main port
* Considered the economic and business center of Morocco
* Home to the enormous Hassan II Mosque, built partly over the water, with a 689-foot (210-meter) minaret topped with lasers directed toward Mecca
* Setting for the 1942 film *Casablanca* starring Humphrey Bogart

Fez

* Second-largest city in Morocco in population
* Oldest part of the city established in the eighth century AD
* World-class leather is produced at the Chaouwara tanneries using methods that have barely changed since medieval times.

The Sahara's dromedary camels have only one hump on their backs and make up about 90 percent of the world's camel population. The rest of the camels have two humps and are called Bactrian camels!

The Sahara

- ✪ The largest subtropical desert in the world, with an area of around 3.3 million square miles (8.6 million square kilometers)

- ✪ Covers part of Morocco, and also Algeria, Chad, Egypt, Libya, Mali, Mauritania, Niger, Sudan, and Tunisia

- ✪ In summer, a hot, dusty wind that originates in the Sahara, the *sharqi,* can drive up temperatures all around the country—to around 105°F (41°C).

CASABLANCA

Casablanca's filled with fascinating things to do and see. Which means that there's lots for VILE to make a grab for in the city—their likely target.

History

* Was once the site of a pirates' haven
* Has been settled or occupied by the Berbers, Portuguese, Spanish, and French
* Site of Franklin D. Roosevelt and Winston Churchill's Casablanca Conference during World War II, where they made plans to fight Nazi Germany

Architecture

* Casablanca is a treasure trove of architecture—from Art Deco to ultra-modern.
* The many Art Deco buildings there are increasingly being protected from demolition.
* The art of zellij (geometric cut-tile patterns) is a hallmark of Moroccan architecture.

Here's looking at you, kid. Keep your eyes peeled for VILE operatives, and I'll meet up with you as soon as I can.

Museums

✱ La Villa des Arts, a gallery housed in an Art Deco building, exhibits art from Morocco and around the world.

✱ Le Musée de la Fondation Abderrahman Slaoui is home to the art collection of a private citizen.

✱ La Fabrique Culturelle des Anciens Abbatoirs is a former slaughterhouse building that now serves as an exhibit, performance, and training space for all kinds of art.

It looks like history is what VILE is after this time. There's an archeological dig in downtown Casablanca that's unearthing ancient artifacts, and a ceramic bowl that was just discovered has gone missing. Can you help Carmen find it?

Ceramic bowl

Paperstar

Origami stars

Pickaxe

Map

Tagine pot

Tiles

Neal the Eel

Great job! But VILE's on the move already. Player will tell you more, and I can catch up with you at our next destination. Let's try to stay close on their tail to see what they're up to.

BRAZIL

BRAZIL

Hi there! Surveillance cameras have picked up VILE operatives in Brazil. It's a long flight, so you have plenty of time to catch up on what you'll find there.

JUST THE BASICS

Population: more than 207 million

Size: 3,227,096 square miles (8,358,140 square kilometers) in area (fifth largest in the world)

Capital: Brasília

Languages: Portuguese and various other languages, including indigenous languages

SHOW ME THE MONEY

Currency: real

Agricultural products: coffee, soybeans, wheat, sugarcane, and cocoa

Industries: shoes, lumber, tin, and steel

WHAT'S FOR DINNER?

Picanha: cut of steak, often served barbecued at all-you-can-eat meat restaurants called *churrascarias*

Coxinha: little chicken fritters made in the shape of drumsticks

Brigadeiros: cocoa and condensed milk truffles

SAY WHAT?

Hello:
olá

Goodbye:
tchau (informal),
adeus (formal)

Other greetings:
bom dia (good morning),
boa tarde (good afternoon),
boa noite (good evening)

What time is it?:
Que horas são?

DANGERS

Creatures:
Brazilian wandering spiders, green anacondas (the world's heaviest snake), piranhas, and golden lancehead viper

BRAZIL

There are a lot of hot spots in Brazil, and many of them are centered around Rio de Janiero. Rio is a sprawling, sometimes beautiful, sometimes gritty, and always amazing city on the east coast of Brazil.

Copacabana Beach

- ✱ One of the most famous beaches in the entire world
- ✱ An expanse of sand around 2.5 miles (4 kilometers) long
- ✱ Site of the 2016 Summer Olympics beach volleyball tournament
- ✱ Hosts one of the world's largest New Year's Eve fireworks shows, attracting roughly two million visitors each year

Cristo Redentor (Christ the Redeemer)

- ✱ Located on top of Mount Corcovado, the statue overlooks Rio de Janeiro.
- ✱ It is 98 feet (30 meters) tall and has an arm span of 92 feet (28 meters).
- ✱ A competition was held to choose a designer for the statue. Construction began in 1926, and last five years.

Favelas

✤ Far above the posh beach neighborhoods in Rio lies a network of about a thousand hillside neighborhoods called favelas.

✤ The first favelas were established in the late 1890s when soldiers returned from war and needed a place to live.

✤ Former African slaves, always in search of affordable housing since Brazil outlawed slavery in 1888, moved there too.

✤ Today, favelas are home to more than 1.5 million Brazilians.

Amazon Rainforest

✤ The world's largest tropical rainforest covering about 40 percent of Brazil's total area

✤ Home to several million species of insects, plants, birds, and other forms of life (with more still to be discovered)

✤ Under threat from deforestation, and shrinking at a fast pace

BRAZIL

Rio is also home to the world's largest Carnival festival. Luckily for VILE, Carnival is in full swing, and there are people everywhere. That will give their operatives the cover they need to get away with something really valuable.

Carnival

- ✺ This yearly festival mixes Portuguese and African traditions.
- ✺ Like Mardi Gras in New Orleans, Carnival is held just before Lent.
- ✺ Street parties called *blocos* take place both day and night.

I'd love to learn how to samba, but there's no time to waste!

Costumes

* Ostentatious creations often featuring sequins and feathers
* Can cost as much as $10,000 for those worn in the Samba Parade

Samba

* Both a kind of music *and* a kind of dancing
* Originally came from African music and traditions and is a vital part of Brazil's culture
* During Carnival, a parade of floats heads through the Sambadrome, each carrying samba dancers in their elaborate costumes.

Stop the party! Or at least take a break from it. Because security cameras have spotted VILE operatives leaving the Sambadrome and heading through the streets of Rio. With them is a Carnival headpiece encrusted with diamonds. Can you find them before they get away? Look for:

Carnival mask

El Topo

Le Chèvre

Brazilian flag

Drums

Guitar

Tigress

Feathers

THE UNITED ARAB EMIRATES

THE UNITED ARAB EMIRATES

It's time to head VILE off at the pass in the United Arab Emirates (UAE). Hope you're not still feeling jet-lagged from your last flight, because there's work to be done and no time to waste. To get you started, here are some tidbits about the UAE.

JUST THE BASICS

Population: more than 9 million

Size: 32,278 square miles (83,600 square kilometers) in area

Capital: Abu Dhabi

Languages: Arabic, Persian, English, Hindi, Urdu

SHOW ME THE MONEY

Currency: Emirati dirham

Agricultural products: dates, vegetables, and watermelons

Industries: petroleum, aluminum, cement, and fertilizer

WHAT'S FOR DINNER?

Khuzi: roasted meat with vegetables and nuts served over rice

Al harees: wheat and meat porridge flavored with cinnamon

Luqaimat: fried sweet dumplings drizzled with date syrup

SAY WHAT?

Hello:
salam (more formal),
marhaba (more casual)

Goodbye:
ma'a salama

Let's go!:
Otanjobi omedeto!

DANGERS

Natural Disasters:
sandstorms and dust storms

Creatures:
scorpions, saw-scaled vipers, and samsum ants

41

Now that you have some of the basics, let's get down to specifics. The UAE is a wealthy country, and you'll find everything from bustling cityscapes to deserts to sandy beaches. There are a lot of places where VILE might strike.

Sheikh Zayed Grand Mosque

- ✿ Opened in 2007 in Abu Dhabi, the burial place of Sheikh Zayed, former president of the UAE

- ✿ Can fit up to 40,000 people at prayer

- ✿ Biggest mosque in UAE and one of the largest in the world, occupying more than 30 acres (12 hectares)

Emirates Palace Hotel

- ✿ Located in Abu Dhabi and has everything from personal butlers to water slides

- ✿ Contains more than a thousand custom-made crystal chandeliers (requiring a full-time staff just to keep them clean)

- ✿ More than 394 rooms in a complex that takes up about 250 acres (100 hectares) of land

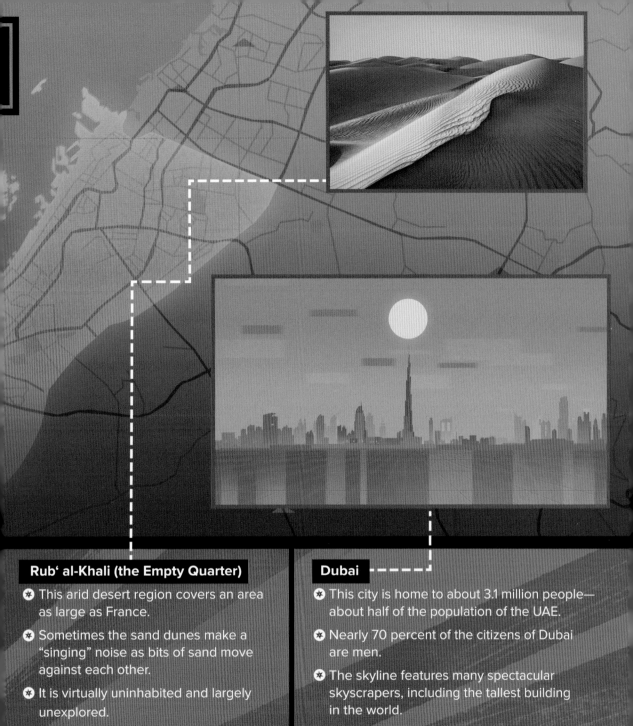

Rub' al-Khali (the Empty Quarter)

✺ This arid desert region covers an area as large as France.

✺ Sometimes the sand dunes make a "singing" noise as bits of sand move against each other.

✺ It is virtually uninhabited and largely unexplored.

Dubai

✺ This city is home to about 3.1 million people—about half of the population of the UAE.

✺ Nearly 70 percent of the citizens of Dubai are men.

✺ The skyline features many spectacular skyscrapers, including the tallest building in the world.

DUBAI

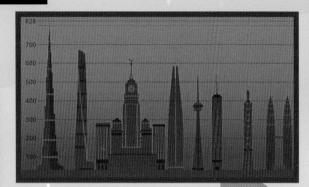

Sounds like Dubai might just be VILE's next target. Let's take a closer look at where they might be heading.

Burj Khalifa

- ✺ This is the tallest building in the UAE—and the entire world!
- ✺ It's got 163 stories (160 are habitable). That's more than 60 stories taller than the Empire State Building.
- ✺ The building's elevator boasts the longest elevator travel distance in the world.

Burj Al Arab Hotel

- ✺ The most luxurious hotel in the world, it has the appearance of a sailboat skimming on the water.
- ✺ Built on a manmade island of sand, with cement columns to hold it steady
- ✺ Has its own helipad and fleet of Rolls-Royces

In 2014, two daredevil skydivers jumped off the top of the Burj Khalifa! That's a high-flying stunt even for me.

Palm Jumeirah

* A manmade archipelago constructed of sand dragged in and heaped up in the water
* Seen from above, it looks like the leaves of a palm tree.
* Islands are connected by a tunnel, bridges, and even a monorail

Dubai Autodrome

* A luxury racetrack in the desert
* Hosts a twenty-four-hour road race (the Hankook 24H Dubai endurance race) each year
* Watch a race or learn to drive a race car yourself on the Autodrome's track.

A gala at the Autodrome is where you're heading, as VILE is already there. There's a new high-tech model race car on display there, and VILE is itching to get their hands on it. Carmen is already on the scene, but she needs your help. So buckle your seat belt and get ready for a wild ride! Look for:

Tire

Racing helmet

Wheel trophy

Neal the Eel

Cup

Tigress

Steering wheel

Tool kit

ITALY

ITALY

Buongiorno! (That's "good day" in Italian.) I wish you had lots of time to sightsee and explore when you get to Italy, but VILE is on the move, so you should be, too. Here's some basic info to get you set up.

JUST THE BASICS

Population: about 62 million

Size: 113,568 square miles (549,970 square kilometers) in area

Capital: Rome

Languages: Italian

WHAT'S THE WEATHER?

Mostly Mediterranean, but in the northern mountains, it's cooler and more alpine. In the far south, it's hot and dry.

SHOW ME THE MONEY

Currency: Euro

Agricultural products: fruits and vegetables, grapes for wine, and olives for olive oil

Industries: machinery, iron, and steel

WHAT'S FOR DINNER?

Pizza: maybe from the world's oldest pizza shop, which is in Naples, Italy

Pasta: various shapes and sauces depending on the region

Gelato: a smooth and silky Italian ice cream

SAY WHAT?

Hello: *buongiorno* (good day) or *buona sera* (good evening)

Goodbye: *arrivederci*

Thank you: *grazie*

Where is the pizza shop?: *Dov'è la pizzeria?*

DANGERS

Natural Disasters: landslides, avalanches, earthquakes, and volcanic eruptions

ITALY

Italy is one of the most culturally rich countries in the world. It was the birthplace of the Renaissance, the seat of the Catholic Church, and so much more.

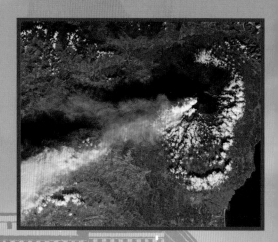

Venice

- A single city made up of 118 little islands in the Venetian Lagoon
- Slowly disappearing into the lagoon as climate change, along with other factors, causes the water level to rise
- Ruled the waterways in this area in times past—and much of the land as well
- Was its own country until 1797, then became part of Austria, and ultimately part of Italy in 1866

Mount Etna

- The most active volcano in all of Europe, located on the island of Sicily on the line where the African and Eurasian geological plates bump against each other
- Has been erupting off and on for at least 500,000 years
- While the ash from its eruptions makes for fertile soil, it's also a source of danger for those who live in its shadow.

Hmm . . . I'd love to see the Sistine Chapel someday. Maybe I can squeeze it in after our mission is over!

The Colosseum

✸ Roman Empire—era amphitheater (a round or oval open-air theater with tiers of seats for spectators)

✸ Opened its doors in AD 80 and still welcomes visitors more than 1,900 years later

✸ It used to host many events, including gory contests between gladiators and wild animals (or other gladiators), mock naval battles, and more. Thankfully, the battling days are over and the Colosseum itself is now the tourist attraction.

Vatican City

✸ Nestled within Rome, this isn't just the headquarters of the Catholic Church— it's also the smallest nation in the world!

✸ Home to the Pope, St. Peter's Basilica, and some of the world's most priceless works of art, including Michelangelo's frescoes on the ceiling of the Sistine Chapel

✸ Has its own post office, flag, and radio station, and mints its own Euro coins

MILAN

There's a lot to see and do almost everywhere in Italy, but you need to head to Milan in northern Italy. The food is great, the architecture is amazing, and—most importantly—VILE is on the loose there.

The Last Supper

- ✪ On view at the monastery of Santa Maria delle Grazie in Milan

- ✪ Huge—about 15 feet (4.6 meters) tall and 29 feet (8.8 meters) wide

- ✪ Leonardo da Vinci painted it using an experimental technique similar to the fresco. The technique was not stable, and the work began flaking after a few years. It has undergone extensive restoration since its completion in 1498.

Duomo di Milano

- ✪ Milan's cathedral took five centuries to build.

- ✪ It's famous for its imposing size, pink marble façade, and 135 spires and pinnacles reaching toward the sky.

- ✪ The great organ in the Duomo has 15,800 pipes ranging from over 30 feet (9 meters) long to only a few inches.

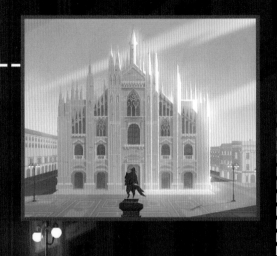

Galleria Vittorio Emanuele II

❉ Named for the first king of Italy

❉ Italy's oldest active shopping mall, built in the late 1800s

❉ Centrally located between two main squares and often referred to as *il salotto di Milano* (Milan's drawing room)

Milan Fashion Week

❉ One of the four major fashion weeks in the world (along with New York, London, and Paris)

❉ Showcases famous (and up-and-coming) fashion designers and models from all over the globe

❉ High-end Italian design houses such as Prada, Versace, Gucci, and Dolce & Gabbana are among those featured.

CALIFORNIA

CALIFORNIA

You may think California is all about Hollywood and making movies, but there's so much more to the state than that . . . as VILE knows all too well—and as you're about to find out!

JUST THE BASICS

Population: about 40 million

Size: 155,779 square miles (403,466 square kilometers) in area

Capital: Sacramento

Languages: English, Spanish, various other languages

WHAT'S THE WEATHER?

Depending on whether you're on the coast or inland, in the mountains or closer to sea level, or in the north or south of the state, the weather changes dramatically.

SHOW ME THE MONEY

Currency: US dollar

Agricultural products: grows a substantial amount of the produce US citizens eat, including almonds, artichokes, citrus fruits, strawberries, tomatoes, lettuce, cauliflower, grapes, and plums

Industries: computers and electronics, chemicals, wine industry, tourism, film and entertainment

WHAT'S FOR DINNER?

Avocado toast

Sourdough bread

Dungeness crab and other seafood

DANGERS

Natural Disasters:
Earthquakes (the state is located on the San Andreas Fault), wildfires, and mudslides

Creatures:
California newts, black widow spiders, ticks, fire ants, and western diamondback and Mojave green rattlesnakes

CALIFORNIA

A big state means a big number of fascinating things to do and see. Is VILE in any of these locations? We'll soon find out!

Big Sur

✷ A region of central California coastline encompassing about 100 miles (160 kilometers) between Carmel and San Simeon

✷ Bordered to the east by the Santa Lucia Mountains and the west by the Pacific Ocean

✷ Showcased by California's Highway 1, known for its winding turns, rugged cliffs, and breathtaking views

Napa Valley

✷ Just north of San Francisco, this area is home to more than four hundred vineyards.

✷ The grapes these different vineyards grow become red, white, and sparkling wines that people drink all over the world.

✷ A railroad was built in 1864 (and is still in use today) to take tourists around the area.

Los Angeles averages about 290 days of sunshine a year—now that's something I could get used to!

Redwood Forests

✪ Redwoods are the tallest trees in the world.

✪ They're also among the longest-living trees in the world, with the oldest clocking in at around two thousand years old.

✪ A redwood named Hyperion—whose location is hidden to protect it—is measured to be the tallest on the planet at about 380 feet (116 meters)—that's taller than the Statue of Liberty!

Los Angeles

✪ Home to Hollywood and known as the entertainment capital of the world with the most production of movies, television, video games, and recorded music

✪ Also has a booming fashion industry, showcased in the high-end shops of Rodeo Drive

✪ The only North American city to have hosted two summer Olympics

✪ Considered to have near perfect weather: abundant sunshine, low humidity, little rain, and mild temperatures

SAN FRANCISCO

But LA isn't your destination today. There's reason to believe that VILE is hiding out in San Francisco, the city by the bay. The fog that rolls off that bay is so dense that the city's residents have given it a name: Karl. So you'll have to contend with Karl the Fog as well as VILE while you're here.

San Francisco

* Home to almost 900,000 people

* Famous for its hilly streets, delicious sourdough bread, and even some sunbathing sea lions down on Fisherman's Wharf

Golden Gate Bridge

* Painted "International Orange," a hue specially made for the purpose

* One of San Francisco's most famous landmarks, with towers that stand 746 feet (227 meters) over the water

* Opened in 1937, and since then has allowed travelers in cars, on bicycles, and on foot to cross the bay in Art Deco style

Cable Cars

* A type of transportation in which cars are pulled on a rail by a continuously moving cable running at a constant speed

* Invented in 1873 by Andrew Hallidie after he observed horses being injured on the city's steep hills

* Before the 1906 earthquake, six hundred cable cars covered about 50 miles (80 kilometers) of the city, but the system was destroyed in the quake and much of it was not rebuilt. Today about three dozen cars still operate on three lines.

Alcatraz

- ✪ An island prison in the San Francisco bay
- ✪ Closed as a prison since 1963, Alcatraz now invites tourists to explore the cells that once held some of the most hardened criminals in the country, including Al Capone.
- ✪ A total of thirty-six men attempted to escape Alcatraz while it was still a prison. All but three were recaptured or died in the attempt (the fate of those three who escaped is still unknown).

Chinatown

- ✪ San Francisco's Chinatown is the oldest in the United States.
- ✪ It was founded around the time of the 1848 gold rush, when Chinese immigrants came to the West Coast looking for work, often facing prejudice and ill treatment when they arrived.
- ✪ The Tien Hau Temple is among the oldest Chinese temples in the US.
- ✪ Chinatown was destroyed by the great earthquake and fires of 1906 and had to be rebuilt.

Chinatown is where you're heading next. There's a prized jade dragon statue that's disappeared, and where better to hide it than among the crowded shops and restaurants in this vibrant neighborhood? You need to find:

Jade dragon

Tigress

Red balloon

Mime

Bomb

Purple paper lantern

Bicycle

cat figure

Umbrella

Nice! You're really good at this. Keep up the impressive work as you travel to our next destination.

ECUADOR

ECUADOR

Have you ever been to Ecuador? That's where I've picked up VILE activity. It's time to try to get acclimated to high altitudes, because Ecuador is a country of towering mountains!

JUST THE BASICS

Population: more than 16 million

Size: 106,886 square miles (276,841 square kilometers) in area

Capital: Quito

Languages: Spanish, Quechua, Shuar

WHAT'S THE WEATHER?

You'll find tropical conditions in the Amazon jungle and along the coast. It gets more temperate as you move into the Andes Mountains.

SHOW ME THE MONEY

Currency: US dollar

Agricultural products: bananas, coffee, cocoa, rice, potatoes, and cassava

Industries: petroleum, textiles, wood products, and chemicals

WHAT'S FOR DINNER?

Llapingachos: cheese and potato patties with peanut sauce

Churrasco: steak served with a fried egg, French fries, rice, plantains, and salad

Quinoa: tiny, grain-like food used throughout the Andes—gluten-free and full of protein

SAY WHAT?

Hello: *hola*

Thank you: *gracias*

Just kidding!: *¡Chendo!*

Goodbye: *adiós*

DANGERS

Natural Disasters: landslides, earthquakes

Creatures: black widow spiders, scorpions, and Africanized (killer) bees

ECUADOR

Ecuador isn't a huge country, but it is home to some of the world's most fascinating animals, like sloths, llamas, caimans, and condors. Which means it is a perfect spot for nature lovers to explore. Since VILE is here too, we'll assume that there's something for non-nature lovers as well.

Galápagos Islands

✪ The inspiration for Charles Darwin's book *On the Origin of Species*

✪ Home to a wealth of animals (many of which can only be found here), including marine iguanas, Galápagos finches, blue-footed boobies, and giant tortoises

✪ Made up of nineteen islands (and even more smaller landmasses) that lie 600 miles (965 kilometers) off the coast of Ecuador

Quito—so beautiful, so likely to give me altitude sickness!

Andes Mountains

- ✪ Run through Ecuador (as well as Venezuela, Colombia, Peru, Bolivia, Argentina, and Chile)
- ✪ Extend along the South American coast for a whopping 5,500 miles (8,850 kilometers)
- ✪ The tallest Andean peak in Ecuador is Chimborazo, at 20,702 feet (6,310 meters).

Quito

- ✪ The second-highest capital city in the world (after La Paz, Bolivia)
- ✪ 9,350 feet (2,850 meters) above sea level
- ✪ Named a UNESCO (United Nations Educational, Scientific and Cultural Organization) World Heritage site in 1978, marking it as a place of international interest

ECUADOR

As amazing as Ecuador's mountains are, the coast is important, too. On the Pacific Ocean, Ecuador's coastal towns and cities are home to commercial fisheries as well as destinations for tourists who want to take fishing excursions.

Coastline

* More than 1,390 miles (2,237 kilometers) of coastline
* Home to resort towns like Salinas with sweeping beaches and beautiful views of the Pacific Ocean
* Popular fishing grounds for yellowfin tuna and marlin
* Great biodiversity of birds and mammals and hot temperatures that appeal to tourists

Guayaquil

* Ecuador's largest city and main port
* Sits about two degrees south of the equator, with a hot and humid climate
* Established in 1537 as Santiago de Guayaquil and named in honor of Saint James (Santiago) and, according to legend, a local chief named Guaya and his wife, Quila

Wildlife

- There are more than 1,500 different bird species on mainland Ecuador.

- Humpback whales pass through the waters off Ecuador during their yearly migration.

- Ecuador's famed pink dolphins—an endangered species—live in the Amazon and other rivers.

Have I mentioned how amazing Ecuador's coast is? It turns out I'm not the only one who thinks so. VILE is near Salinas, where a local fisherman found a three-hundred-year-old shipwreck—and some jewels that went down with it. Now VILE wants those jewels. Can you help find them before VILE does? Here's what to look for:

Treasure chest

Orange cat

Yellowfin tuna

Le Chèvre

El Topo

Compass

Fishing rod

Diamond

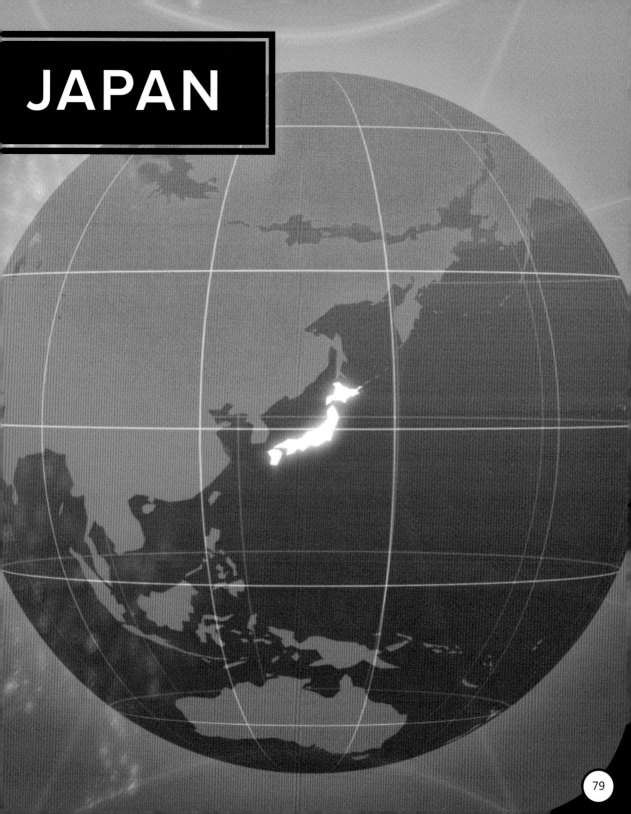

JAPAN

JAPAN

Yokoso (that means "welcome") to Japan, a country made up of thousands of different islands, though some of them are definitely a lot bigger than others. Here's what you need to know.

JUST THE BASICS

Population: more than 126 million

Size: 140,728 square miles (364,485 square kilometers) in area

Capital: Tokyo

Languages: Japanese

SHOW ME THE MONEY

Currency: yen

Agricultural products: vegetables, rice, tea, sugarcane, fruits, beef

Industries: cars, electronics

WHAT'S FOR DINNER?

Sushi: raw fish with rice and seaweed

Kabayaki: grilled fish, usually eel, glazed with a sweet sauce

Daifuku: chewy rice dough balls with a filling inside, usually red bean paste

SAY WHAT?

Hello: *konnichiwa*

Thank you: *arigato*

Goodbye: *mata ne*

Happy Birthday!: *Otanjobi omedeto!*

DANGERS

Natural Disasters:

earthquakes, tsunamis, volcanoes

Creatures:

giant hornets—can be 1.5 to 2 inches (3.8 to 5 centimeters) long

JAPAN

I put together some other information about Japan to help you get acclimated.

Islands

* Japan stretches over approximately 1,500 miles (2,400 kilometers) and more than 6,000 different islands. Most of the population, though, lives on the four largest islands: Honshu, Hokkaido, Kyushu, and Shikoku.

* These islands have been occupied by humans for tens of thousands of years.

* Japan, one of the most geologically unstable places in the entire world, experiences roughly a thousand tremors annually. Most are minor, but huge earthquakes (and the resulting tsunamis) have struck the country.

Mount Fuji

* This volcano is located only about 60 miles (96 kilometers) from Tokyo.

* It is considered active by geologists, though it hasn't erupted since 1707.

* At 12,388 feet (3,776 meters) tall, it's also the country's tallest mountain.

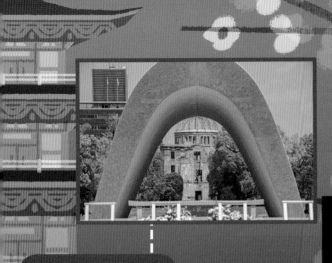

> The cherry blossoms appear for only a few weeks, so let's just stop and smell the—oh, wait a minute! VILE is on the move. They didn't come to smell the flowers, so neither can we.

Tokyo

* ❀ Located on the island of Honshu, Tokyo is Japan's capital city, as well as its political, economic, and cultural center.

* ❀ Tokyo's subway system carries around 8.7 million commuters a day, making it one of the busiest in the world.

* ❀ Central Tokyo is home to more than 9 million people.

* ❀ The emperor of Japan resides in the Imperial Palace, the seat of Japan's royal family, right in the heart of the city.

Cherry Blossoms

* ❀ The cherry blossom is the national flower of Japan and has spiritual significance in Buddhism.

* ❀ Each spring, Japan celebrates the blooming of the cherry trees all over the country with a festival, Sakura Matsuri.

Hiroshima

* ❀ The city was destroyed when the US dropped the atomic bomb on Hiroshima at the end of World War II (August 6, 1945).

* ❀ An estimated 80,000 people died on impact, and radiation exposure from that day killed more than 100,000 people in the years afterward.

* ❀ The Hiroshima Peace Memorial includes the only building left standing where the bomb hit. It serves as a reminder of the horrors of war and the need for peace and hope.

Carmen's right: VILE didn't come to smell the flowers—though they're seriously missing out! There's a special exhibit of samurai swords at the Tokyo National Museum, and one of them just went missing. Surveillance cameras show that VILE operatives have already escaped and are heading out to the streets! Now it's up to you to find the stolen samurai sword, an important piece of Japanese history, as well as to try to apprehend everyone from VILE who was involved in this operation. What you need to find:

Rainbow backpack

Lady Dokuso

Moose Boy

Waraji sandals

Sushi

Cherry blossom

Otter Man

Samurai sword

Whew—that was a close call! Good work collecting the missing sword. I wish we had time to stop for a sushi roll, but Otter Man and Moose Boy got away. Where are they heading next? Player's got the intel.

INDONESIA

INDONESIA

This time, VILE hasn't traveled so far. They're headed to Indonesia—which is made up of more than seventeen thousand (yes, you read that right) different islands—and they've got a head start on you. I've done some quick research to get you settled in.

JUST THE BASICS

Population: more than 260 million

Size: 699,451 square miles (1,811,569 square kilometers) in area

Capital: Jakarta

Languages: Bahasa Indonesia, English, Dutch, and Javanese

WHAT'S THE WEATHER?
Tropical—hot and humid.

SHOW ME THE MONEY

Currency: Indonesian rupiah

Agricultural products: rice (around 70 million tons of it each year), palm oil, cocoa, coffee, and rubber crops

Industries: petroleum, natural gas, clothing, and shoes

SAY WHAT?

How are you doing?: *Apa kabar?*

Thank you: *terima kasih*

What time is it?: *Jam berapa?*

See you later: *sampai jumpa*

WHAT'S FOR DINNER?

Satay: grilled meat skewers served with peanut sauce—usually a street food

Ikan Bakar: grilled fish with chili and soy sauce

Klepon: rice balls with a palm sugar liquid in the center, rolled in coconut

DANGERS

Natural Disasters: earthquakes, tsunamis, and more than a hundred active volcanoes

Creatures: komodo dragons—(the world's largest lizard, growing up to 10 feet/ [3 meters] long and 300 pounds/ [136 kilograms])—cone snails, sea wasp jellyfish

INDONESIA

> With so many islands, we have to try to focus our search. Here are some places VILE might be staking out.

Java

- ✺ Location of Jakarta, the nation's capital
- ✺ Only the fourth-largest island of Indonesia, but home to more than half the country's population
- ✺ Last refuge of the one-horned Javan rhinoceros at Ujung Kulon National Park on the island's westernmost tip

Rice Fields

- ✺ Indonesia is the world's third-largest producer of rice.
- ✺ The country produces more than 70 million tons (75 million metric tons) of this staple food per year.
- ✺ Most rice farming is wet rice cultivation, in which seedlings are planted in flooded fields.

Hopefully conservation efforts will help build Sumatran orangutan populations back up. We don't want this amazing species to go extinct!

Volcanoes

* ✪ Mount Krakatoa on Rakata Island had one of history's great eruptions in 1883—so loud that it could be heard in Australia.

* ✪ Mount Agung, the highest point in Bali, erupted in 1963 after being dormant for 120 years.

* ✪ Mount Ijen in east Java emits sulfur gas that combusts on contact with air and turns into a liquid, which can look like blue lava flowing down the mountain.

Sumatra

* ✪ The sixth-largest island in the world and the second-largest Indonesian island, after Borneo

* ✪ Has some of the most diverse natural forests as well as one of the worst deforestation rates in the world

* ✪ Vegetation includes the monster flower (*Rafflesia arnoldii*), the largest known individual flower of any plant species in the world

* ✪ One of the only places in the world where the critically endangered species orangutans (the word means "people of the forest") live in the wild

JAKARTA

There's so much to explore in Indonesia, but my data says that VILE is in Jakarta, so you need to be there, too!

Jakarta

- Just as New York City is called the Big Apple, Jakarta is called the Big Durian after a native fruit (which, incidentally, smells like gym socks).

- It's the biggest city in Indonesia, with about 10.5 million people.

- Roughly 40 percent of the city is below sea level.

- Like much of the Java coastline, it's being threatened as the Java Sea rises due to climate change and the land sinks due to groundwater drilling.

A master of shadow puppetry is known as a *dalang*. It's one of those *dalang*'s festivals that VILE seems to be targeting.

Pasars (Markets)

* Have everything from fruits and vegetables, to meats and fish, to clothes and shoes

* Textile *pasars* offer different fabrics and patterns depending on what island of Indonesia you are on.

* Pasar Baru is one of the oldest markets in Jakarta, established in the 1800s, though its name literally translates to "new market."

Wayang Museum

* One of several museums to be found off Fatahillah Square at the center of Jakarta's Old Town

* A museum celebrating shadow puppetry, an art form that's over a thousand years old

* Shadow puppetry is an important part of Indonesian culture, with festivals performed around Jakarta and elsewhere in Indonesia.

The word on the street is that the Wayang Museum is lending a five-hundred-year-old shadow puppet to a festival that starts tonight. It's a priceless piece of Indonesian history, and VILE is after it. Can you find the shadow puppet before it disappears along with the VILE operatives?

Shadow puppets

Le Chèvre

Gong

Durian fruit

Drums

Bamboo flute

Kite

El Topo

Awesome job! But I'm hearing from Player that VILE is heading out of Indonesia already.

NEW YORK

NEW YORK

It's a long trip from the Big Durian to the Big Apple, but New York is where VILE has turned up. Here's some information about the state of New York for you.

JUST THE BASICS

Population: about 20 million (the fourth largest in the US)

Size: 47,126 square miles (122,057 square kilometers) in area

Capital: Albany

Languages: English, Spanish, various other languages

WHAT'S THE WEATHER?

Like much of the northeastern US, it can be cold in winter and hot in summer—and how extreme either gets depends on where you live.

SHOW ME THE MONEY

Currency: US dollar

Agricultural products: apples (it isn't called the Big Apple for nothing: the state is the second-biggest grower of apples in the country), dairy, hay, corn, and maple syrup

Industries: finance, insurance, real estate, health care

WHAT'S FOR DINNER?

Pizza

Bagels with cream cheese

Hot dogs   Clam chowder

Cheesecake

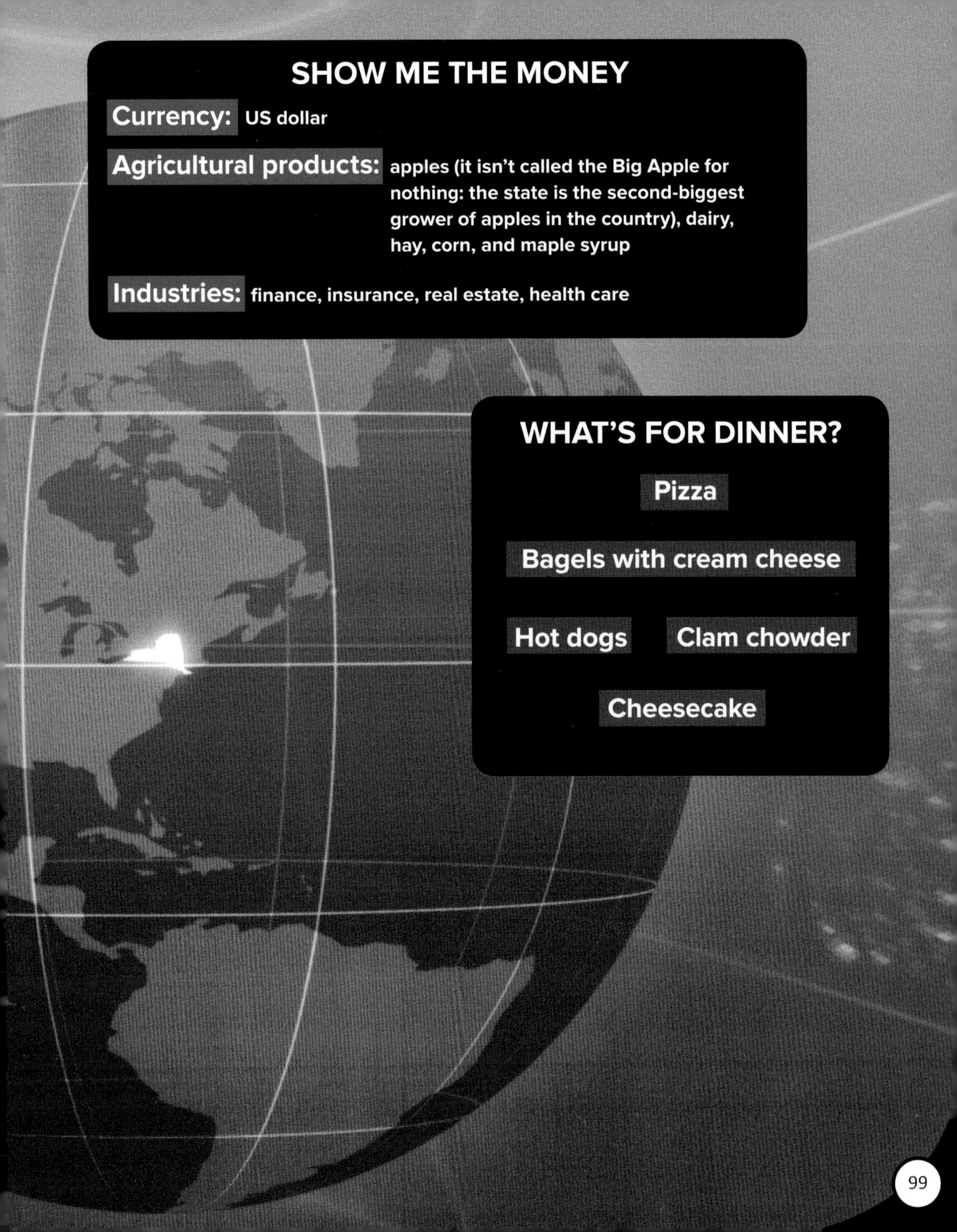

NEW YORK

When you hear "New York," you might just think about the city. But there's a whole lot happening all over the state. And with so much going on, who knows where VILE will strike?

Albany

* New York's capital city
* Located on the Hudson River about 150 miles (241 kilometers) north of New York City
* Named by the English for the Duke of Albany in 1664, previously known as Beverwijck, or "beaver district," to the Dutch, and Pempotowwuthut-Muhhcanneuw, or "the fireplace of the Mohican Nation"

Long Island

* Long Island is 118 miles (190 kilometers) long and 23 miles (37 kilometers) wide at its most distant points—that's bigger than the state of Rhode Island!
* The Long Island Rail Road is the oldest railroad still operating under its original name in the US, and is also the busiest commuter railroad in North America.
* Long Island is home to more than twenty-five lighthouses.

I've never been to Niagara Falls, but I hear that people used to go over the falls in barrels and other contraptions in times past (which doesn't sound like a good idea to me)!

New York City

- ✲ Settled by the Dutch in the seventeenth century and called New Amsterdam

- ✲ Passed into English colonists' hands in 1664 and received its current name

- ✲ Manhattan, one of the five boroughs that make up New York City (the others are Brooklyn, Queens, the Bronx, and Staten Island), takes its name from the Native Americans who lived on the island until European colonists took it over.

- ✲ Today, New York City residents come from all over the world, and scholars estimate there might be as many as eight hundred different languages spoken there.

Upstate and Western New York

- ✲ Upstate and western New York have rolling hills, dramatic cliffs, and even Niagara Falls if you go all the way to the Canadian border.

- ✲ Visit the long, narrow Finger Lakes, where you'll find natural wonders like Watkins Glen State Park and its Gorge Trail.

- ✲ Travel west to the shores of Lake Erie and Lake Ontario.

NEW YORK

No reason to worry about going over Niagara Falls, because the big city seems to be where VILE is heading! And being home to almost nine million people across New York City's five boroughs, it's not going to be easy to track down VILE.

Times Square

- ❂ Chock-full of glowing billboards, taxis, and tourists—one of the big destinations in the city

- ❂ Shares a neighborhood with Broadway and the theater district. (So you can buy some souvenirs and then head to see an award-winning play, all within a couple of blocks!)

- ❂ Most famous place in the US to spend New Year's Eve, with live music and the "ball" dropping at midnight

Statue of Liberty

- ❂ Statue designed by Frédéric-Auguste Bartholdi, and supported by an interior scaffolding made by Alexandre-Gustave Eiffel (the same guy who designed the Eiffel Tower)

- ❂ A gift from France to the United States that has stood beside Ellis Island since the late 1800s, a sign of liberty and welcome to immigrants, tourists, and locals

- ❂ Torch covered in sheets of twenty-four-karat go

There's no question this stroll through the park was fantastic, but heads up: VILE's on their way to the library!

Empire State Building

✸ The world's tallest structure when it was built

✸ Stands 102 stories tall

✸ In the movies, the giant gorilla King Kong famously climbed up the side of the building, but you can just take elevators up to the observation deck.

Central Park

✸ Spans 843 acres (341 hectares) in the center of Manhattan

✸ Took the effort of about twenty thousand workers—and lots of gunpowder to blast through huge rocks and stones—to build it

✸ First opened in 1859 and today has a zoo, venues for theater productions and concerts, its own waterways, an ice skating rink, and more

The two lions that guard the doors to the New York Public Library, Patience and Fortitude, didn't even notice the whole team of VILE operatives sneaking into—and out of—the library. But security has reported that five letters from the Revolutionary War have gone missing! Can you find the letters before it's too late? Here's what to find:

Map

Binoculars

Hat

Tigress

Green book

Toy lions

Five antique letters

Lady Dokuso

Pigeon

Bag

You did it! You're no longer a potential thief—you're a full-fledged part of my crew. With all the information you gathered from Player, you managed to stop VILE in their tracks. And it's not too shabby that you also stole back some priceless artifacts and treasures from all around the world.

You may not have noticed, but I was with you the whole time. Go back to all the places you visited and see if you can find me.

And keep in mind: VILE is still out there, and I may need to call on you again in the future. So keep your ears open and your eyes peeled—you never know when a thief in a red fedora might come knocking on your door again!

ANSWER KEY